W9-CAX-572

SUPER FLY GUY

Tedd Arnold

CARTWHEEL BOOKS

An Imprint of Scholastic Inc.

For Little Tate William
—T. A.

No part of this publication may be reproduced, stored in a retrieval system, or transmitted in any form or by any means, electronic, mechanical, photocopying, recording, or otherwise, without written permission of the publisher. For information regarding permission, write to Scholastic Inc., Attention: Permissions Department, 557 Broadway, New York, NY 10012.

ISBN 978-0-439-92300-2

Copyright © 2006 by Tedd Arnold. All rights reserved. Published by Scholastic Inc. SCHOLASTIC, CARTWHEEL BOOKS, and associated logos are trademarks and/or registered trademarks of Scholastic Inc.

18 17 16 15 14 13   16 17 18 19/0

Printed in the U.S.A.   40

This edition first printing, April 2014

A boy had a pet fly.
The fly was named Fly Guy.
Fly Guy could say the boy's
name—

Chapter 1

One day Fly Guy went
to school with Buzz.

Fly Guy learned about
reading and phonics.

He learned about art.

Then it was lunchtime.
Fly Guy loved the lunchroom.

He loved the dirty dishes.

He loved the smelly mop.

He loved the garbage cans.

Fly Guy met the lunch lady.
Her name was Roz.

"No flies in the lunchroom!" Roz said. Fly Guy said—

ROZZz!

"This fly is smart," said Roz.
"He knows my name!"

She fed Fly Guy chicken bones
and fish heads in sour milk.
Fly Guy was happy.

Chapter 2

Roz's boss was not happy.
"The children cannot eat
in a room full of flies!"
he said. "You are fired!"

Roz was sad. Fly Guy was sad. Buzz and the children were sad because Roz was a good cook.

The next day, Roz was gone.
Miss Muzzle was the new
lunch lady.

She made burnt peas and turnips. No one in school ate lunch—not even Fly Guy, who ate almost anything.

Everyone missed Roz.
Even the boss missed Roz.

That night, Buzz made a plan.

Chapter 3

The next day, Fly Guy went to school again. In the lunchroom Fly Guy said—

Miss Muzzle looked up.

Fly Guy boinked her on the nose.

Miss Muzzle cried, "No flies in my lunchroom!"

She grabbed her swatter
and swung. She missed.

She missed again.

She missed again.

She missed again.

She missed again.

The boss was not happy.
"The children cannot eat
in this mess," he said.
"You are fired!"

The next day, Roz was back.
"You are a super Fly Guy!"

Roz made a special garbage soup for Super Fly Guy.

Fly Guy was happy.

Everyone was happy.